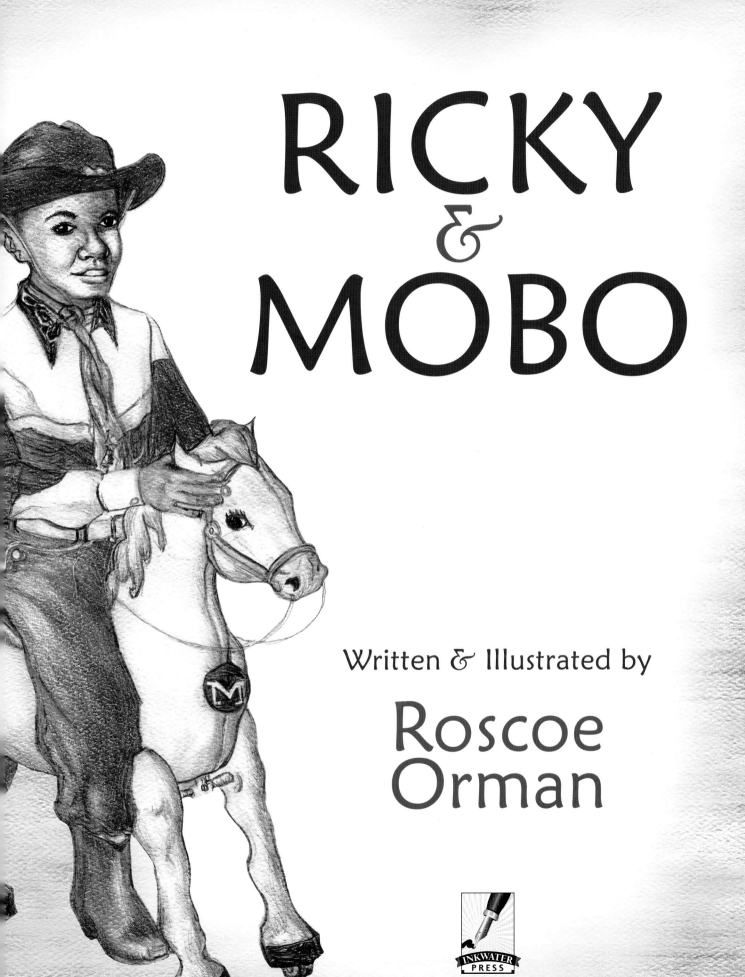

RICKY & MOBO

Written & Illustrated by

Roscoe Orman

INKWATER PRESS

It was the morning of June 11th, 1950, Ricky's sixth birthday, and when he woke up, he could hardly believe his eyes.

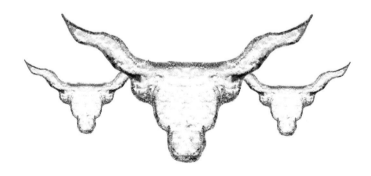

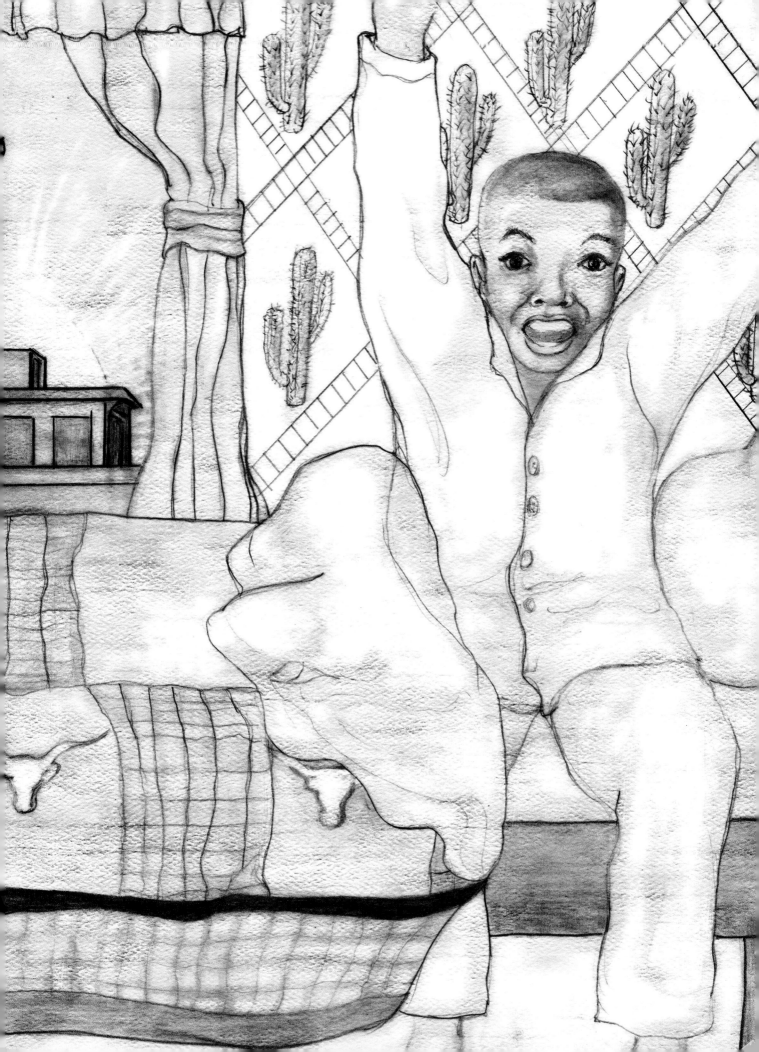

Standing at his bedroom door
was the best present he had gotten in his
whole life – a gleaming white toy horse
he could ride on! Mobo was his name.
Mobo! Mobo! Mobo! Wow! Ricky loved
his new toy horse, Mobo.

For Ricky, Mobo was the next best thing
to having a real live horse. Mobo was
perfect since the apartment Ricky lived in
with his parents and his sister Cookie was
too small for a real horse.

Mobo had little rubber wheels under his black hoofs, and when Ricky pumped his feet in the stirrups the white metal stallion would roll forward, stopping only when Ricky pulled back on the reins just like his cowboy heroes on TV.

For days after that, Ricky hardly moved from room to room without riding his trusty horse. From his bedroom to the kitchen to the living room and back, it was Ricky and Mobo.

Like Roy Rogers
and Trigger,

like
The Lone Ranger
and Silver,

like peanut butter and jelly,

they were inseparable.

A few weeks after Ricky's birthday, his mom announced, "Guess what? There's going to be a big block party for the whole neighborhood next week right here on Stebbins Avenue."

"They're going to have food and music and all kinds of games for the kids. And, oh, best of all, the day will end with a big race for kids up to the age of seven."

Ricky thought for a minute. "What kind of race, Mommy? A running race?"

"No, Ricky, the rules say you can race with anything on wheels but no motor: skates, scooters, tricycles, or whatever other riding toy you might have."

"Wow," shouted little Ricky, "Do you think maybe I can ride Mobo in the race, Mommy? Please, please?"

His mother smiled one of those big wide grins that always meant "yes": "Of course you can, Ricky. That's exactly what I was thinking."

Ricky shouted as loud as he could, "Yay, yay, yay. I'm gonna race Mobo!"

Ricky could hardly sleep for the next five days, and when he did, he dreamt about racing Mobo across the plains of the Wild West.

After what seemed to Ricky like forever, the day of the block party finally came. And what a day it was!

The sky was a beautiful deep blue with puffs of cottony white clouds a mile high. A sparkling sun glowed beyond the building tops. And on the street, the air was electric with the excitement of the day's events.

It seemed as though every man, woman, and child from all the surrounding neighborhoods had come to Stebbins Avenue. People Ricky had never even seen before greeted him and everyone else as if they were long-time friends.

The day's festivities began with food and music. Kids and grownups danced in the street. And then came the contests and games, like double-dutch jump rope, dominoes, and hopscotch.

At last, the time had come for the big race. All of the racers were told to gather at one end of the block. The race was to the other end of the block and then back again to the starting line.

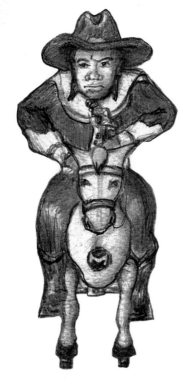

Ricky rode Mobo to the front of the two rows of racers. Mobo stood out as the only horse among all the roller skates, scooters, tricycles, fire trucks, and other varieties of home-made vehicles.

This was much farther, Ricky thought, than he had ever ridden Mobo before. But he was too excited to worry or doubt his chances of winning. "This," he thought, "is going to be the greatest day of my life."

Mr. Gaines, who owned the corner candy store, raised his starter pistol and shouted,

"On your mark."

Ricky's sweaty hands gripped Mobo's reins.

"Get set."

Ricky scrunched down into the saddle to get a good first pump on the stirrups.

"Go!"

Ricky had hardly heard the word "go" before he realized that most of the racers were already on their way down the block. He began to pump the stirrups, slowly at first, then faster, faster, until, finally, he felt like one of his cowboy heroes racing his stallion across the open plains.

Ricky's heart was racing even faster than his pumping feet, and the roar of the cheering crowd spurred him on even more, until he almost felt as if he and Mobo had wings.

Then, all of a sudden, Ricky looked up and saw that a whole bunch of racers—skaters and cyclists and scooter riders—were all heading toward him, back to the finish line.

He didn't dare stop and look back to see if anyone was behind him. Instead, he pumped even faster. Ricky was determined to close the huge gap between himself and the others, who were getting close to the finish line. "C'mon, Mobo," he whispered into the horse's ear.

Finally, he reached the end of
the block. As he turned Mobo
around to head back, just as
he had feared, the two of them
were all alone.

For a moment he thought, "Why
don't I just quit?"

But he looked up and saw the entire streetful of spectators cheering for him and Mobo to "go, go, go." Ricky's heart was in his throat, pounding like a drum. He took a long, deep breath, buried his chin into his chest, and aimed his trusty horse toward the finish line.

Now the race belonged only to them. No more competition. No winning or losing. Just the joy of crossing the finish line!

Ricky heard those cheers in his head for days, weeks, and even years to come. And whenever he did, he felt special and proud, because on that day he and Mobo were truly champions.

Because on that day he had learned one of life's most valuable lessons: that you can still be a winner in the race, even when you come in last.

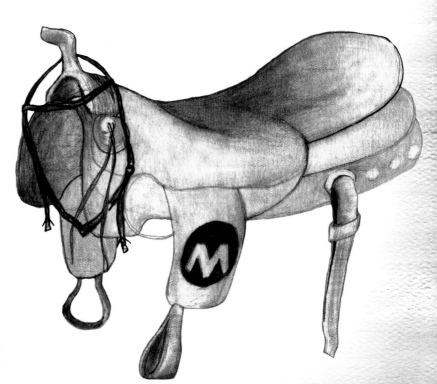

THE END

Roscoe Orman is an award-winning actor who is known to millions for his thirty-three-year portrayal of Gordon Robinson on the highly acclaimed children's television series *Sesame Street*. Orman is a Bronx native and graduate of New York's High School of Art & Design, Circle-In-The-Square Theatre School, and Manhattan School of Music and made his professional acting debut in the 1962 musical revue *If We Grow Up*. A forty-five-year veteran of over sixty theatre productions for Broadway, Off-Broadway, and regional theatres, he has also performed a wide range of roles in film and television. He has toured throughout the United States, Canada, and the Caribbean with his *Gordon of Sesame Street Concert* series and with Matt Robinson's one-man play *The Confessions of Stepin Fetchit*. An accomplished performer, director, teacher, poet, writer, illustrator, and lecturer, in 2006 Orman wrote his memoir, *Sesame Street Dad: Evolution of an Actor*, published by Inkwater Press. He and his wife Sharon reside in New Jersey, and are the proud grandparents of five.

"I am thrilled to share the story of *Ricky & Mobo* with all of you kids. It's a true story from my own childhood. I hope you will enjoy reading it or having it read to you. I believe that each of you will find the *champion* inside of you and learn to love the journey of becoming the best that you can be and to never give up in the race of life."

~ Roscoe Orman,
also known as "Gordon" of *Sesame Street*

Cover and interior design by Masha Shubin
Leather texture © Nick Schlax, iStockPhoto.com

Library of Congress Cataloging-in-Publication Data

Orman, Roscoe, 1944-
Ricky & Mobo / written and illustrated by Roscoe Orman.
p. cm.
Summary: When six-year-old Ricky rides his toy horse, Mobo, in a race during a
block party, he learns that one does not have to be the fastest to be a winner.
ISBN-13: 978-1-59299-255-3 (hardcover : alk. paper)
ISBN-10: 1-59299-255-2 (hardcover : alk. paper) [1. Racing--Fiction.
2. Toys--Fiction. 3. Parties--Fiction.] I. Title. II. Title: Ricky and Mobo.
PZ7.O6337Ric 2007
[E]--dc22
2007004208

The Mobo Bronco, a ride-on toy horse, was produced by D. Sebel & Co. of Kent, England,
from 1947 to 1972. The company's New York City office opened in 1948.

www.inkwaterpress.com

ISBN-13 978-1-59299-255-3
ISBN-10 1-59299-255-2

Publisher: Inkwater Press

Printed in China
All paper is acid free and meets all ANSI standards for archival quality paper.